STANDARDS-BASED LEARNING & FUN!

THEODORE ROOSEVELT
AND TURN-OF-THE-CENTURY AMERICA

Primary Sources

20 Primary Sources!
We dug through the archives so you don't have to!

For the work of a day,
For the taxes we pay,
For the Laws we obey,
We want something to say.

GLOBE—SATURDAY, MAY 28, 1898.
BILL OF FARE
CUBA STEAK
PORTO RICO PIG
PHILIPPINE FLOATING ISLANDS
SANDWICH ISLANDS
WELL, I HARDLY KNOW WHICH TO TAKE FIRST!

ACADEMICS' CHOICE™ SMART BOOK AWARD WINNER

TEACH IT TODAY! CORE RESOURCE™

by Carole Marsh

THE ROUGH RIDERS.

THEY ARE ROUGH ON THE SPANIARDS, WHETHER THEY RIDE ͻR WALK.

Courtesy of Library of Congress

Cover of *Puck* magazine shows Theodore Roosevelt leading the Rough Riders into battle against the Spanish in Cuba during the Spanish-American War – 1898

Courtesy of Library of Congress

Political cartoon satirizing the concept of American imperialism at the turn of the century – 1898

Courtesy of Wikimedia Commons

Republican campaign poster for the 1900 U.S. presidential election – features President William McKinley and vice presidential candidate Theodore Roosevelt – 1900

Courtesy of E.T. Paull Music Company

Sheet music cover for "Dawn of the Century" March and Two Step – depicts optimism about a better future through progress in technology – 1900

Courtesy of Library of Congress

Photograph of a woman dressed in male attire and smoking a cigarette supervising a man doing laundry – depicts the changing role of women – 1901

COPYRIGHT 1900, PAN-AMERICAN EXPOSITION CO.
BIRDSEYE VIEW OF THE PAN-AMERICAN EXPOSITION, BUFFALO, MAY 1 TO NOVEMBER 1, 1901.
BY HARRY FENN AFTER DRAWINGS BY CARRERE & HASTINGS, N.Y.

Courtesy of Library of Congress

Illustration of Pan-American Exposition (World's Fair) in Buffalo, New York – 1901

Courtesy of Library of Congress

Artist's conception of the shooting of President William McKinley at the Pan-American Exposition – McKinley later died of his wounds and Theodore Roosevelt became president – 1901

Courtesy of Wikimedia Commons

Political cartoon depicting President Roosevelt's "Big Stick" foreign policy: "Speak softly, and carry a big stick." – 1904

Courtesy of Library of Congress

Cover of *Judge* magazine showing Theodore Roosevelt wearing an allegorical crown of the Panama Canal, "the greatest achievement for trade in modern times" – 1904

Courtesy of Library of Congress

Political cartoon depicting a Standard Oil tank as an octopus wrapping its tentacles around steel, copper, and shipping industries, as well as the U.S. Capitol and the White House – 1904

Courtesy of Library of Congress

Photograph looking down Sacramento Street in San Francisco after the 1906 earthquake

Courtesy of National Museum of the USAF

Photograph of Orville Wright flying the 1908 Flyer at Fort Myer, Virginia – 1908

Courtesy of William Charles Morris, Spokesman-Review Cartoons

Political cartoon featuring the many roles Theodore Roosevelt filled during his lifetime – 1908

"PROTECT AND PRESERVE THE REMAINING FORESTS UPON PUBLIC LANDS FROM DEVASTATION AND DESTRUCTION, WHICH HAVE BEEN THE FATE OF THOSE IN FOREST SECTIONS OF THE COUNTRY."
REHSE

A PRACTICAL FORESTER
(A subject that had attention all through Mr. Roosevelt's Presidency.)
From the *Pioneer Press* (St. Paul)

Courtesy of St. Paul Pioneer Press

Editorial cartoon depicting President Roosevelt's conservation policies to protect wilderness and wildlife – 1908

Courtesy of Library of Congress

Political cartoon depicting Uncle Sam, George Washington, and Theodore Roosevelt greeting the Great White Fleet as the ships returned to Virginia after a cruise around the world – 1909

Courtesy of Library of Congress

Photograph depicting an example of child labor in early 1900s – children working as spinners in a Mississippi yarn mill – 1911

Courtesy of Library of Congress

***Titanic* ready for launch – 1911**

Courtesy of NOAA

***Titanic's* bow when shipwreck discovered in 1985**

Photographs of the RMS *Titanic* – the British passenger liner sank in the North Atlantic Ocean after hitting an iceberg in April 1912

VOTES FOR WOMEN
For the work of a day,
For the taxes we pay,
For the Laws we obey,
We want something to say.
6342

Courtesy of Library of Congress

Postcard depicting sentiments of the women's suffrage movement – 1913

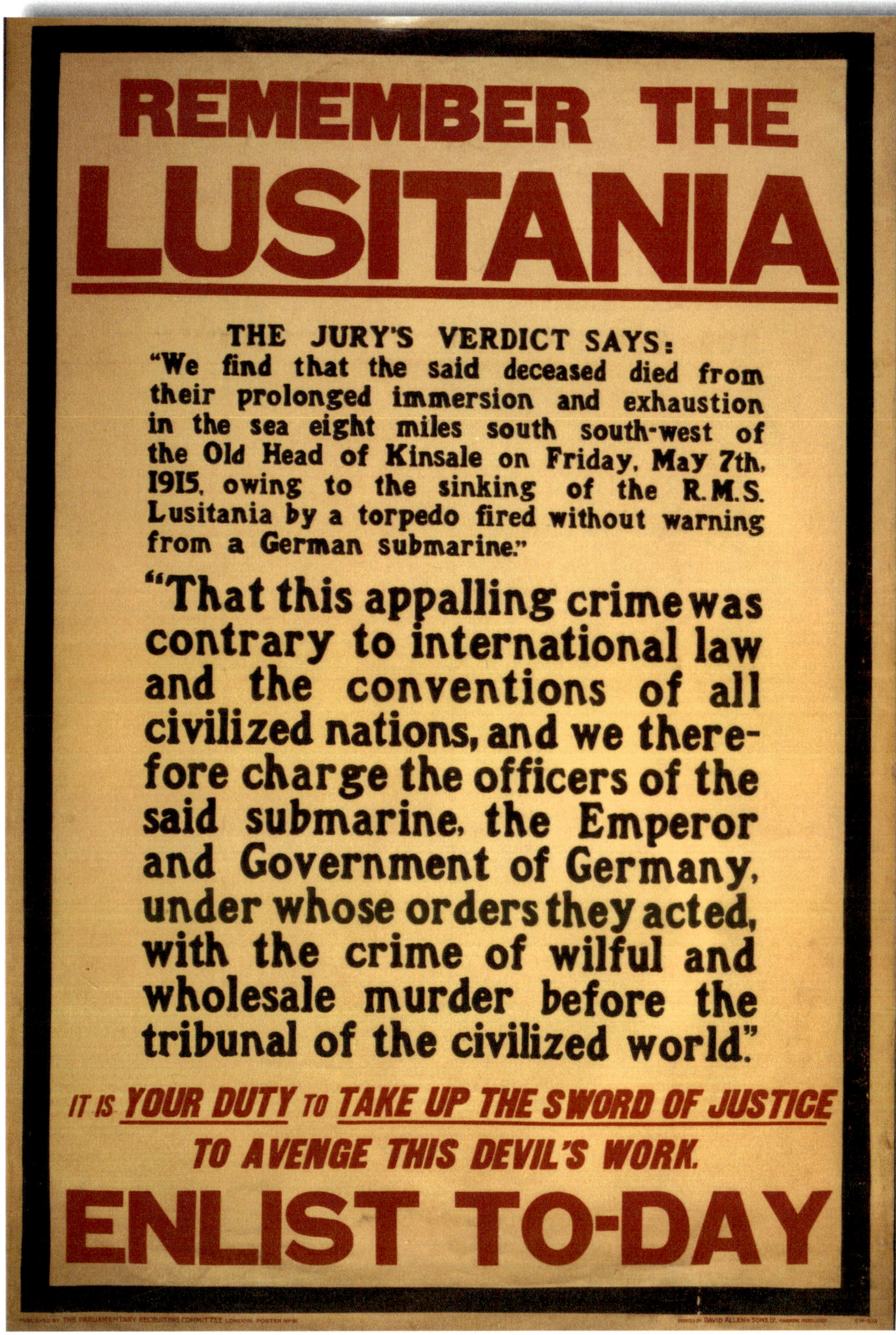
REMEMBER THE
LUSITANIA
THE JURY'S VERDICT SAYS:
"We find that the said deceased died from their prolonged immersion and exhaustion in the sea eight miles south south-west of the Old Head of Kinsale on Friday, May 7th, 1915, owing to the sinking of the R.M.S. Lusitania by a torpedo fired without warning from a German submarine."
"That this appalling crime was contrary to international law and the conventions of all civilized nations, and we therefore charge the officers of the said submarine, the Emperor and Government of Germany, under whose orders they acted, with the crime of wilful and wholesale murder before the tribunal of the civilized world."
IT IS YOUR DUTY TO TAKE UP THE SWORD OF JUSTICE
TO AVENGE THIS DEVIL'S WORK.
ENLIST TO-DAY

Courtesy of Library of Congress

Poster urging citizens to remember people killed on the RMS *Lusitania* and enlist in the military – the British ocean liner was sunk by a German U-boat in 1915 – the sinking was a factor influencing the United States to enter World War I in 1917 – poster dated 1915

Courtesy of National Park Service

Photograph of Mount Rushmore National Memorial in South Dakota – the sculpture features George Washington, Thomas Jefferson, Theodore Roosevelt, and Abraham Lincoln – photo taken 2010

THEODORE ROOSEVELT
AND TURN-OF-THE-CENTURY AMERICA
Primary Sources

Historical Documents • Maps • Photographs • Political Cartoons

INCLUDES 20 PRIMARY SOURCE DOCUMENTS:

- Cover of *Puck* magazine shows Theodore Roosevelt leading the Rough Riders into battle against the Spanish in Cuba during the Spanish-American War – 1898
- Political cartoon satirizing the concept of American imperialism at the turn of the century – 1898
- Sheet music cover for "Dawn of the Century" March and Two Step – depicts optimism about a better future through progress in technology – 1900
- Photograph of a woman dressed in male attire and smoking a cigarette supervising a man doing laundry – depicts the changing role of women – 1901
- Artist's conception of the shooting of President William McKinley at the Pan-American Exposition – McKinley later died of his wounds and Theodore Roosevelt became president – 1901
- Political cartoon depicting President Roosevelt's "Big Stick" foreign policy: "Speak softly, and carry a big stick."– 1904
- Cover of *Judge* magazine showing Theodore Roosevelt wearing an allegorical crown of the Panama Canal, "the greatest achievement for trade in modern times" – 1904
- Political cartoon depicting a Standard Oil tank as an octopus wrapping its tentacles around steel, copper, and shipping industries, as well as the U.S. Capitol and the White House – 1904
- Photograph looking down Sacramento Street in San Francisco after the 1906 earthquake
- Photograph of Orville Wright flying the 1908 Flyer at Fort Myer, Virginia – 1908
- Political cartoon featuring the many roles Theodore Roosevelt filled during his lifetime – 1908
- Editorial cartoon depicting President Roosevelt's conservation policies to protect wilderness and wildlife – 1908
- Political cartoon depicting Uncle Sam, George Washington, and Theodore Roosevelt greeting the Great White Fleet as the ships returned to Virginia after a cruise around the world – 1909
- Photograph depicting an example of child labor in early 1900s – children working as spinners in a Mississippi yarn mill – 1911
- Photographs of the RMS *Titanic* – the British passenger liner sank in the North Atlantic Ocean after hitting an iceberg in April 1912
- Postcard depicting sentiments of the women's suffrage movement – 1913
- Poster urging citizens to remember people killed on the RMS *Lusitania* and enlist in the military – the British ocean liner was sunk by a German U-boat in 1915 – the sinking was a factor influencing the United States to enter World War I in 1917 – poster dated 1915
- Photograph of Mount Rushmore National Memorial in South Dakota – the sculpture features George Washington, Thomas Jefferson, Theodore Roosevelt, and Abraham Lincoln – photo taken 2010

Perfect for Gallery Walks & Literature Circles!

Build Higher-Order Thinking Skills:

- Analysis
- Critical Thinking
- Point of View
- Compare and Contrast
- Order of Events
- & Much More!

FREE 15-page Online Teacher's Guide!
www.gallopade.com/pstg

GALLOPADE

www.gallopade.com
Printed in Peachtree City, GA

ISBN-13: 978-0-635-12593-4 $17.99